FINGER LAKES PHOTOGRAPHY

The images of John Francis McCarthy are available as art prints suitable for framing from Finger Lakes Photography, Skaneateles, New York. Stop in to see us or you may visit the gallery online at www.johnfrancismccarthy.com. If you wish to be notified in advance of the release of the next book, please leave us your email address at the web site.

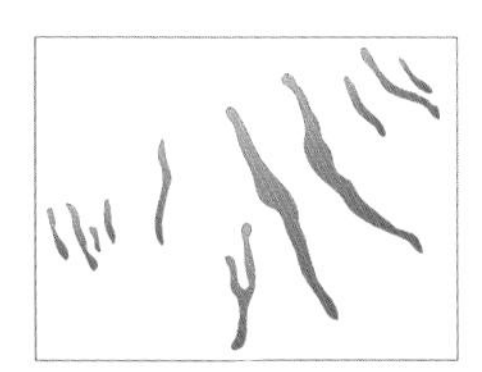

Published by:
Finger Lakes Photography, Skaneateles, New York 13152
315-685-9099 www.johnfrancismccarthy.com

©2007 by John Francis McCarthy. All rights reserved.

Book Design: Cooper Productions
Printed by: Finger Lakes Press, Auburn, New York

ISBN 978-0-9632716-7-7

Welcome To Skaneateles

Skaneateles Lake was a short ride for me from Tipperary Hill on Syracuse's west side where I grew up. The images were imprinted long ago on countless Sunday's spent touring apple orchards near Skaneateles Village and picnicking on Sandy Beach, where for a dollar a family could stake out a few yards of beautiful shoreline.

The 42-mile ride from the village around the lake includes short diversions to Carpenter's Falls, New Hope Flour Mill, Millard Fillmore's boyhood home site and the rustic Glen Haven Hotel. Road signs like Mandana, New Hope, Sempronius, Scott and Borodino delight the eye and trigger the imagination.

We usually begin the trip on West Lake Road where one can appreciate the beauty and dimension of the lake almost immediately. The road begins its gentle rise from West Lake Street for about a mile to the first of several magnificent views.

At Mandana, six miles down the road, is a restaurant and a marina. A mile south there is a second spectacular view, a true panorama, where rolling hills give way to high cliffs on the lakeshore.

At 11 miles, the road to Apple Tree Point crosses atop Carpenter's Falls, one of many east-west escarpments from stream and glacial erosion that formed the Finger Lakes. Most of the waterfalls around the lake are on private property.

Carver Road, off Apple Tree, leads to the site of Millard Fillmore's boyhood home. Our 13th president once taught at the district school in Scott. Picnic tables offer an opportunity to enjoy rich and scenic farmscapes before visiting New Hope Mill and winding down into Glen Haven.

Traveling south from Fillmore's, Carver intersects Glen Haven Road. A right turn brings us back to New Hope, home of the New Hope Flour Mill built in 1823 and operated continuously since. The mill, one of the last year-round grist mills left in New York State, produces a variety of pancake mixes. It is one of the largest overshot water wheels in the eastern US.

From New Hope, the road to Glen Haven, lined with tall trees and wildflowers, drops quickly to the lakeside. Watch for the old Pennsylvania railroad car that has been converted into a summer camp, and the site of the Glen Haven Sanatorium (1841-45), one of America's pioneer water cures. Dr. W. C. Thomas, its founder, lived 107 years.

Across the lake from the sanatorium site is the Glen Haven Hotel and Marina, offering lake access for boaters and fishermen. From the hotel parking lot one can enjoy another spectacular panoramic view – especially in late June when the sun sets in the northwest and reflects eight miles down the lake.

From Glen Haven the road winds south to Scott and East Lake Road for the trip back to the village. The road rises quickly from Scott to one of the highest elevations in the county and the best reason for traveling the lake from west to east. At the crest of the hill is the quintessential view of Skaneateles Lake and ample space to pull off the road and enjoy it. We named it the "Homecoming View."

Leaving the overlook, the road north, with its farms and lake views, lulls us into thinking that the best views are behind us. Soon travelers are surprised to discover another spectacular view from The 1820's House, a converted farmhouse now a restaurant.

At Borodino, a mile north of the summit, is a public golf course and restaurant. A left turn off the main road leads to Lourdes Camp. A right turn leads to Otisco Lake and Marcellus.

For the final seven miles to the village, the road drops to lake level and sprawling farmland gives way to residential areas.

Bring your camera when you tour the lake. Don't hesitate to stop along the way to talk to people. Ask questions. There are characters here and stories and secret places that few people have seen. If you're lucky you will hear about them. If you're truly fortunate, you'll be invited to visit them.

From 500 feet above the village taken from Bruce Silvers powered parachute.
Riding above the lakes with Silvers proved to be an exhilarating adventure.

The setting sun reflecting off the clouds lights up the main sail. After a trip around the world, President Lincoln's Secretary of State, William H. Seward called Skaneateles Lake "the most beautiful body of water in the world."

The Margaret Chase Gazebo reflects the pride of the community as the Judge Ben Wiles awaits a new wave of passengers. An early morning visit this tranquil and scenic lake park is a wonderful way to begin the day.

Late summer afternoon view from West Lake Street.

Carpenter's Falls. This 90-foot waterfall is one of several in a magnificent gully that empties into Skaneateles Lake.

Sunday polo match.

From Silver's aircraft looking north along the west shore.

Skaneateles Country Club.

Overnight snowfall. To my delight, while viewing this image I discovered that a formation of Canada Geese had been captured in the frame.

Scrooge and the Piper add color and sound to the annual 'Dickens' Christmas' celebration.
Dickens wrote of how clear it was to him that "one is driven by irresistible might until the journey is worked out!"

Sherwood Inn. Built as a stagecoach stop in 1807, the Sherwood is a favorite resting place for travelers and locals. To me, a visit to the tavern is the quintessential Skaneateles experience.

St. James Episcopal Church.

Winter brings out the ice fishermen.

Closed for the season.

Sundown at the country club.

Sunrise at the village pier.

Spring colors in full bloom.

A summer morning at Wickwire Point looking south to Glen Haven.

A perfect day for sailing.

Life along the inlet at Glen Haven.

Grazing horses.

New Hope Mills above Carpenter's Falls.

The Homecoming View. When travelers heading north reach this point on the east side of Skaneateles Lake they realize they are in the Finger Lakes region again.

A golden sunrise reveals the beauty of ice and snow on the lake.

Old Pump House. Years ago, when the north shore of the lake was closer to the country club than the village, this building housed the machinery to control the level of the lake.

A Saturday evening performance at Brook Farm, home of the Skaneateles Festival of classical music.

At Brook Farm, musicians live, eat, rehearse, relax and perform as guests of the Robinson family, co-founders of the Festival.

Morning on West Lake Street.

Each winter when a great cloud forms on the lake, I usually get a call.
That is all the encouragement I need.

Sunrise on Main Street. Sometimes it's just a matter of standing in the right place to get the shot.

The John D. Barrow Gallery, an annex to the Skaneateles Library, opened in 1900 and houses more than 300 paintings of this respected American artist.

Marina on the southwest shore.

A rainbow on Main Street.

Five Lakes Sunset. View from 2500 feet. Winter sun reflects across Seneca, Cayuga, Owasco, Skaneateles and Otisco lakes.
The opportunity to capture this image lasted just a few seconds before the clouds gathered and darkened the landscape.

Looking south over the Skaneateles watershed high above Glen Haven.

Fog on the country club road.